Bark, Bark, Bark!
Let's Go to the Doggy Park

Written By
Karen Anderson-Hurd

Bark, Bark, Bark! Let's Go to the Doggy Park
Copyright © 2023 by Karen Anderson-Hurd

All rights reserved. No part of this publication may be reproduced, distributed, or transmitted in any form or by any means, including photocopying, recording, or other electronic or mechanical methods, without the prior written permission of the author, except in the case of brief quotations embodied in critical reviews and certain other non-commercial uses permitted by copyright law.

Tellwell Talent
www.tellwell.ca

ISBN
978-0-2288-7642-7 (Hardcover)
978-0-2288-7641-0 (Paperback)

Thanks to "The Dog Bar" and to the Owner, Steven for allowing me to use their logo; being that it has been a Miami institution on Lincoln Road for nearly thirty years! I must also thank my wonderful Friends and their incredible young children for giving me input and fun ideas to incorporate into this book. Also, to my friend, Sara and to the JW Sexsmith Elementary School here in Vancouver for affording me the opportunity to read to the young students in Ms. Nanda's class. To my Mother-in-Law, Kathy, who graciously assisted me as well my Father, Fred, who Helped me when I needed to find that one key word! Thank You to my husband, Sean for listening to me reading my book aloud and for championing me in getting this book to completion. Thanks again to everyone who believed in me (you know who you are) Lisa, Maria, Laura, Robin, Sarah, Erica, Tanis and Priscilla....And of course, my beloved chihuahua, Alexander Anderson, who was a very small doggy with a really Big heart!

Acknowledgements

...And thanks to a Friend who worked at our Miami Beach vet; it's because of her that Alexander + Sophia even met! And now, it seems to be one of the cutest Chihuahua love stories yet.

So if You are thinking about getting a new puppy, whether it's adopting, fostering or rescuing a doggy as your pet...

We hope that you remember this little story about friendship because it is one that we will be sure to never forget.

Alexander + Sophia they met at the park
Every time they see each other, they go bark, bark, bark!

Sophia catches Alexander by tugging on his shirt, then they both tumble to roll around in the grass and the dirt!

At the doggy park,
there are lots of different dogs to see

Sometimes, these two pups like to sit under the **big**, giant tree.

Other times, there are big dogs playing, jumping and fetching a ball

While Sophia sees Alexander running and chasing them all!

One sunny afternoon,
five dogs showed up for a **fiesta**

They played the entire day, then went home for a L-o-n-g siesta!

The next day, Alexander didn't want to play with Sophia at all,

But it was... only because he had just got a shiny new toy ball.

The ball was blue, and Sophia had one, too!

But her ball was yellow and bright pink, **I think...**

After the doggy park, sometimes they hit the beach for a little more fun.

Where they frolic around, playing in the sand in the warm Miami sun!

But their favorite spot is the doggy park; it's where they first met,

Which is why these two pups like to go there, every chance that they get!

And every time they go, there's new dogs to greet,
But they stick together, which is kind of sweet!

And speaking of sweet, these pups love something fun to eat
So,
on the way home,

they get to have their yummy treat!

These two chihuahuas love going to the park,
But they always go home before it gets dark.

And at the end of the day, when it's time to sleep
Aah... they both are so quiet; you won't hear a peep!

About the Author

Karen Anderson-Hurd is an American-Canadian author. She was born and raised in Ft. Lauderdale, Florida, making her a native Floridian. She has a Bachelor of Arts degree in English Literature & Writing from FSU. She also studied on the London Program in England and is well-traveled, having been to more than 50 countries. Karen has lived in London, UK; Vancouver, Canada as well as in New York City and in Miami Beach, Florida.

She lived in Miami Beach for nearly twenty years and has always loved living by the ocean, being immersed by the tropical Art Deco style that is so bold and iconic, which is portrayed throughout this colorful book.

Over the years, she has written and published several articles in magazines, but this is her first children's book. This book is written as a narrative poem to tell a story because of its simple rhyme scheme. This is great for young readers because it's easy to keep the pace where the words and sentences share the exact assonance and number of syllables, making it much more fun for them to read.

Karen currently lives in Vancouver, Canada, with her husband and their rescue dog named Marley. And she has already finished writing her next book, which is also about another fun-loving pup!

Printed in the USA
CPSIA information can be obtained
at www.ICGtesting.com
LVHW060227241223
767302LV00017B/244